fenway
AND THE
LOUDMOUTH BIRD

fenway
AND THE
LOUDMOUTH BIRD

VICTORIA J. COE

illustrated by
JOANNE LEW-VRIETHOFF

putnam

G. P. PUTNAM'S SONS

For Rose —V.J.C.

Be free, Papa, we love you forever 'n' ever —J.L.V.

G. P. PUTNAM'S SONS
An imprint of Penguin Random House LLC, New York

First published in the United States of America by G. P. Putnam's Sons,
an imprint of Penguin Random House LLC, 2023

Text copyright © 2023 by Victoria J. Coe
Illustrations copyright © 2023 by Joanne Lew-Vriethoff

G. P. Putnam's Sons is a registered trademark of Penguin Random House LLC.
Penguin Books & colophon are registered trademarks of Penguin Books Limited.

Visit us online at penguinrandomhouse.com.

Library of Congress Cataloging-in-Publication Data
Names: Coe, Victoria J., author. | Lew-Vriethoff, Joanne, illustrator.
Title: Fenway and the loudmouth bird / Victoria J. Coe; illustrated by Joanne Lew-Vriethoff.
Description: New York: G. P. Putnam's Sons, 2023. | Series: Make way for Fenway!
Summary: "Fenway is flabbergasted when he meets a bird who speaks Human, and he
is even more surprised when they actually become friends"—Provided by publisher.
Identifiers: LCCN 2022006936 (print) | LCCN 2022006937 (ebook)
ISBN 9780593406977 (hardcover) | ISBN 9780593406984 (paperback) | ISBN 9780593406991 (epub)
Subjects: CYAC: Jack Russell terrier—Fiction. | Dogs—Fiction.
Cage birds—Fiction. | LCGFT: Animal fiction.
Classification: LCC PZ7.1.C635 Ft 2023 (print) | LCC PZ7.1.C635 (ebook) | DDC [Fic]—dc23
LC record available at https://lccn.loc.gov/2022006936
LC ebook record available at https://lccn.loc.gov/2022006937

Printed in the United States of America

ISBN 9780593406977 (hardcover)

ISBN 9780593406984 (paperback)

1st Printing

LSCC

Design by Marikka Tamura | Text set in Bodoni Six ITC Std

CONTENTS

1. NANA'S . . . 1

2. MERLIN . . . 11

3. GOODBYE, TREATS . . . 21

4. THE BELL . . . 29

5. SQUIRRELS . . . 37

6. BACON! . . . 47

7. ALONE . . . 57

8. THE SEARCH . . . 65

9. PLOP-JINGLE-JINGLE . . . 73

10. FRIENDS . . . 79

1

NANA'S

As soon as my short human, Hattie, opens the car door, I hop outside. My ears are perked. My nose is high. And my tail is wagging.

I hear a lawn mower. I smell the faint aromas of coffee, licorice, and a little bit of cherry. And I see sidewalks, grass, and rows of buildings.

I know this place!
It's where Nana lives!
"Hooray! Hooray!"
I bark. "We're visiting Nana!" I
run in circles, twisting the leash
around Hattie's legs.

I love Nana! Nana
snuggles my neck. She
rubs my belly. She plays
my favorite game,
abracadabra!

That's when Nana holds a little ball, covers it with a silky scarf, and says, "Abracadabra." She pulls the scarf away and pretends she can't find the ball. I know it's under Nana's sleeve, but I sit perfectly still. I've learned that if I act like I don't know where it is, she gives me a yummy treat.

Now I know why I smelled a bag of treats in the car. Yippee! Me and Nana are going to play the abracadabra game! I can hardly wait!

Fetch Man and Food Lady head up one of the walkways. They

chatter away, sounding as excited as I feel. Hattie, too. "Aw, Fenway," she says. She giggles and untangles my leash.

"Let's go, Hattie!" I bark, chasing after the Tall Humans. "I want to see Nana! Right now!"

When we get to the end of the walkway, I stop to water an oak tree. It smells like sneaky squirrels, and I think I hear a few up in the branches. But I can't bark at squirrels now. I need to get to Nana. I haven't seen her in a long, long time!

Fetch Man strides up to the

building beside the tree. I hear a buzz and then a garbled voice. "Come on," he calls to us as the door swings open.

"Whoopee!" I bark. We're here! We're really at Nana's! I rush through the door and lead Hattie up the stairs that smell like Nana.

I speed down the hallway. I make a sharp turn at the open door, and—

"Nana!" I bark, jumping on her legs. "I'm so happy to see you!"

Nana laughs. Her eyes crinkle on the outside and sparkle on the inside. Her long hair hangs over her shoulder, dark and silvery. She

squats down, and we rub noses. "Aw, Fenway," she says.

I leap higher. "Are we going to play the abracadabra game now?"

But Nana has something else on her mind. When she's finished hugging everyone, she ushers us

7

into a room with a couch and comfy chairs. And right away, I smell trouble.

A bird is in the house!

Birds belong outside. With squirrels.

Nana leans her head close to a big cage on a stand. "Merlin, say hello."

The bird pecks her hair. He turns to us and opens his beak. "HELLO!"

2

MERLIN

Whoa! Are my ears playing tricks on me? Or did that bird just speak . . . *Human*???

"HELLO!" he says, bobbing his head.

"Wow!" Hattie laughs and claps her hands. So do Fetch Man and Food Lady. They can't take their eyes off the cage.

Nana's grin is as big as her whole face. "Good boy, Merlin!"

Merlin spins around. "HELLO-HELLO-HELLO!"

My fur prickles. This is not right. Birds aren't supposed to speak Human words. They're supposed to sing bird songs.

And birds are also not supposed to be the center of attention. That's what dogs are for.

"Nana, Nana!" I bark, romping back and forth. "Get that bird outside where it belongs so we can play the abracadabra game!"

Nana stays focused on the cage. So does everybody else.

And that loudmouth bird keeps shouting, "HELLO-HELLO-HELLO!"

They're acting like the bird belongs here. I have to try something else. I paw Nana's legs. "Remember the game we played last time?" I bark. "Abracadabra?"

Maybe she doesn't. Nana gives me a quick pat and turns right back to the cage.

I look around. This is no fun.

Everyone watches as Nana pokes a finger through the bars. The bird hops onto it like he's done this a million times. He takes a little bow.

"Cool!" Hattie cries. She takes
a little ball off Nana's shelf. A silky
scarf and a thin stick, too. She
covers the ball with the scarf.

Hooray! Hattie's going to play

the abracadabra game with me!
I'm so ready!

But instead of looking at me,
Hattie leans in beside Nana. She
presses her face against the cage.
"Merlin, say 'abracadabra'!"

What?! Is it *his* game now?

Nana stares at Hattie like she's
not sure this is a good idea.

Hattie taps the top of the cage
with the stick. "Say 'abracadabra.'"

Everybody gapes at the bird
even though he's just perched on
Nana's finger. Doing
absolutely
nothing.

"Ab-ra-ca-dab-ra," Hattie says slowly. "Come on, Merlin."

Merlin opens his beak. "ACK! Abracadabra! Abracadabra! ACK!"

Hattie bounces. "Yes! Attaboy, Merlin!" She pulls the scarf away and shows Nana her empty hand.

Food Lady and Fetch Man whoop and clap.

I drop down for a scratch. This is a disaster. I glance around the room. It reminds me of our Lounging Place at home. The other end of it looks a bit like our Eating Place.

The Eating Place? Wait a minute! I know why Nana's not playing the abracadabra game with me—the treats are still in the car!

I rush over to the door and give it a furious scratch. "Open up!" I whine. "We need to get the treats!"

"FEN-way!" Food Lady scolds. Uh-oh. That's how the humans tell me "You're in trouble."

"FEN-way! FEN-way! FEN-way!" the bird screeches in that same "you're in trouble" voice. "FEN-way! FEN-way! FEN-way!"

Him, too?! This visit to Nana's is not going the way it's supposed to. I paw at the door. "Get me out of here!"

3

GOODBYE, TREATS

Hattie sighs loudly and rushes to the door. She clips on my leash. Yes! She gets it!

When we burst into the hallway, I notice Fetch Man and Food Lady are following us. Nana, too.

They're not trying to stop us, are they?

I can't take any chances. Those

treats are too important. So is getting away from that loudmouth bird who keeps scolding me for no reason. I lead Hattie to the end of the hall and down the stairs. There's no time to waste.

Outside, we head down the walkway. We're halfway to the parking lot when my ears perk.

CHIPPER-CHATTER-SQUAWK!

I leap up, my tail on alert. Those sounds can only mean one thing—a sneaky squirrel!

CHIPPER-CHATTER-SQUAWK!

I whip around. Aha! I spot him scampering around the oak tree, heading in our direction. "Get away from my short human!" I bark. "Or else!"

He glares at me. And doesn't move. Who does he think he's dealing with?

I need those treats. But nothing's more important than protecting Hattie. "Scram, Rodent!" I bark.

CHIPPER-CHATTER-SQUAWK!

Yikes! A second squirrel darts across the path of the first one. Now they're both after Hattie!

My head swivels. If I weren't on this leash, I'd . . . I'd . . .

"Fenway," Hattie groans.

What's she upset about? I'm only doing my job.

Fetch Man and Food Lady breeze past us. Nana's beside them, chatting excitedly. They're almost at the parking lot. They're probably going to get the treats!

What great news!

I'd better go help. I turn back to the squirrels and bark, "You're getting off easy this time, Rodents.

But I'm warning you—stay away from my short human."

One of them chitters. The other flicks his tail. I have a feeling this business is far from over.

But first things first. "Time to go, Hattie." I steer her toward the parking lot.

Food Lady and Nana are hugging. Fetch Man is opening the car door.

I quicken my pace. I knew it! He's going to get the treats!

"Hooray! Hooray!" I bark, jumping on Fetch Man's legs. "I'm so ready for those treats."

He reaches down and rubs my head. "Aw, Fenway," he says. Then he wraps his arms around Hattie and kisses her cheek.

"Come on," I bark.

But instead of pulling out the bag, Fetch Man slides into the car and closes the door. Wait a minute!

I lead Hattie around to the other side of the car. I paw Food Lady's knee. "Don't forget the treats," I bark.

Food Lady bends over and pats my back. "Be good," she says. She pulls Hattie into a hug and rocks her back and forth.

Next thing I know, the car roars to life, and Food Lady pops inside. She waves her arm out the window as the car drives off . . .

With the treats.

4

THE BELL

I have to catch that car! I jump and twist, but it's no use. Even if Hattie wasn't holding the leash, I couldn't run that fast. The car is gone. And so are the treats.

Hattie leads me back up the walkway. She does not seem the least bit concerned that Fetch Man and Food Lady left. Neither does Nana.

Inside, I settle onto the mat by the door. I growl under my breath. Something's wrong, and I need to figure out what it is.

Hattie and Nana put on capes. They take turns stuffing the scarf into their fists and saying that word: "abracadabra." Why? There's no ball. There's no job for me. And no treats.

Right when I think things can't get worse, Hattie and Nana go over to the cage. Nana points to a shiny bell beside the bird's little swing. "Abracadabra!" she cries.

Merlin pecks
the bell with his
beak and—

DING-DING-DING!

Ouch! That sound hurts my ears!

DING-DING-DING!

Merlin opens his beak. "ACK! Abracadabra! Abracadabra! ACK!"

Hattie swishes her cape. She laughs, and taps the cage with the stick. "Abracadabra!" she says.

Merlin pecks the bell over and over. *DING-DING-DING!* *DING-DING-DING!* *DING-DING-DING!*

I can't just lie here and watch. I have to do something!

I leap up

and rush over to Hattie. I jump on her legs. I nip at the cape. It slides from her shoulders. "Don't you want to play with your adorable dog?" I bark.

"Fenway," she says, pushing me down.

"FEN-way! FEN-way! FEN-way!" Merlin repeats. "FEN-way! FEN-way! FEN-way!"

I growl at the cage. "Cut it out!"

Hattie scoops me into her arms. Squeezing me tight, she holds me

up near the big cage and points at the bird.

Merlin pecks at her finger. "FEN-way! FEN-way! FEN-way!" he cries.

"Hey, leave her alone!" I bark.

"Fenway, shhh," Hattie says in her serious voice. "Friends."

If I didn't know better, I'd think she was trying to get me to be friends with Merlin. Like that could ever happen! How could a dog and a bird be friends anyway? It's not like we could play together. Plus, this guy is the opposite of friendly. He's the one using the "you're in trouble" voice.

"FEN-way! FEN-way! FEN-way!" he cries again.

"Stop that!" I bark.

Hattie sighs and sets me down. She puts the cape back on.

For the rest of the afternoon, I hide under the couch. Hattie and Nana play the totally-not-fun abracadabra game with that bird. He doesn't seem to want treats, only that annoying bell. And that's when I figure out what's wrong.

EVERYTHING.

5

SQUIRRELS

Later, Hattie and Nana are washing dishes in the Eating Place when I hear horrible squawking sounds outside the big window. I must investigate!

I hop onto the couch and press my snout against the glass. My fur bristles with alarm. Sneaky squirrels are scurrying through the

branches of the oak tree right outside. They're probably trying to
come into Nana's apartment.

"Go away, Rodents!" I bark.
"This place is off-limits!"

Even though I'm barking my loudest, they don't seem to listen. They just keep scampering along the branch as if there isn't a fierce dog on the other side of this big window.

I growl. I claw the glass. I bark some more. "I said, 'Go away!'"

A groan sounds behind me. Loud footsteps, too. Hattie comes rushing over. "Fenway," she scolds.

I've been hearing that "you're in trouble" voice way too often today. What's up with that?

Nana says something to Hattie

that I can't understand. But she must be asking about the dangerous threat, because Hattie answers, "Squirrels."

"SQUIRRELS!" Merlin cries from the cage.

Whoa! Even he understands the terrible danger we're in. I claw the glass some more. "Beat it!" I bark at the squirrels.

"Fenway," Hattie grumbles. Her hands close around my belly, and she carries me away.

I kick my legs, craning my neck toward the window. "What are you doing?" I bark. "I was trying to protect you!"

"Here," Hattie says. She grabs the little ball from the shelf.

"I was in the middle of a very important job, Hattie," I bark, wiggling to get free.

Hattie sets me on the rug and rolls the ball across the floor. "Go get it, Fenway!" she sings in a very excited voice.

It's not the abracadabra game, but playing ball is fun, too. I'm about to chase after it when—

"SQUIRRELS!" the bird cries again.

I leap up, my hackles rising. I knew I couldn't take a break! I fly back onto the couch. "Scram,

Rodents!" I bark. "Or you'll get it!"

I gaze out the window. I don't see any squirrels. But that doesn't mean they're not sneaking around.

"SQUIRRELS!" Merlin yells. "SQUIRRELS! SQUIRRELS!"

Hattie scoops me up again. Nana closes the blinds. Now I can't see what's happening outside. How will I know if the squirrels keep trying to attack?

When it's dark, me and Hattie snuggle on the couch with pillows and blankets. Nana spreads her cape over Merlin's cage and kisses us good night.

I close my eyes . . .

Me and Nana are playing the abracadabra game. She covers the little ball with the scarf. I want to get the ball so badly, but I need to wait. Because the treat is coming!

Except it isn't. There are no treats. Instead, a bell rings. A squirrel squawks.

This is no fun!

I rush around Nana's apartment. "We need treats!" I bark. "Where are the treats?"

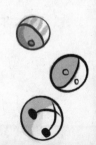

I search
everywhere.
The bell keeps
dinging and dinging.
My legs are so tired. My
bark is wearing out. But
I won't give up . . .

. . . *because I smell a wondrous scent— BACON!*

And I get the Best Idea Ever!

6

BACON!

When I open my eyes, Nana's apartment smells like bacon! But before I can follow the smell into the Eating Place, Hattie takes me out for a walk.

Normally, going on a walk is almost as exciting as bacon, but all we do is pace in front of the oak tree. I barely have time to bark at a squirrel before we head back inside.

Then I remember the bacon! As soon as my leash is off, I rush over to the counter. "Bacon, please!" I bark.

"Aw, Fenway," Nana coos. She bends down and snuggles my neck.

I lick her fingers. *MMMMM!* They taste like bacon!

Hattie sits at the table, and Nana brings over plates piled high with food. I'm right on her heels.

While the two of them eat maple-y pancakes and bacon, I plop myself at Hattie's feet. I look up at her with the cute face she likes. Now I know why she wasn't concerned about those treats that were left in the car. Bacon is the Best Treat Ever! I can't wait to play the abracadabra game with bacon!

But despite my efforts, the yummy meat stays on top of the table.

When Hattie and Nana bring their plates to the sink, I see my opportunity. I leap onto Hattie's chair and—

CHOMP!

Wowee!!! *MMMMM!*

Hattie spins around. "Fenway!" she yells.

Hey, what did she expect?

"FEN-way! FEN-way!" Merlin screams from the big cage in the Lounging Place. What's it to him if I helped myself to a little bacon? Or all the bacon.

Hattie scoops me up and follows Nana back to the Lounging Place. We watch as Nana moves Merlin into a smaller cage on top of the bookcase.

Merlin bucks and flutters. He must not like the smaller cage. And who could blame him? All his

toys and snacks are still in the big one.

While Merlin protests in the smaller cage, Nana carries the big cage to the Eating Place and calls us over. Hattie is very interested in whatever Nana is about to show her.

So am I.

Nana takes all the things out of the big cage and plops them into the sink. Water whooshes in.

I can hear Merlin flitting around in the smaller cage. "FEN-way! FEN-way!" he keeps yelling, like I'm the one who took his stuff away.

"Cut it out!" I bark.

"Fenway, shhh!" Hattie scolds.

He's the one making the racket!

"FEN-way! FEN-way!" Merlin screams again.

I thrash in Hattie's arms. "Make him stop! Make him stop!" I bark.

But he won't. There's only one thing to do. I duck my head under Hattie's arm. I can still hear Merlin fussing and yelling, but at least it's not as loud.

After a few minutes, the whooshing water stops, and Hattie backs away from the sink. I stick my head out, and my eyes bulge in surprise. Nana's carrying the big cage back to the Lounging Place. It smells a lot cleaner for some reason.

Nana sets the cage on the high stand and goes back to the sink. She returns with Merlin's things, putting a food bowl, a water bottle, the bell, and something that looks like dried flowers into the fresh cage.

Nana goes over to the bookshelf. Before she opens the door

to the smaller cage, she gives me and Hattie a warning look. Hattie clutches me tighter to her chest. It seems like a strange time for snuggling, but I won't complain.

Merlin climbs onto Nana's finger. He raises his wings and glares at me.

As Nana places him back into the big cage, I wiggle out of Hattie's arms and bump into the stand. "What are you glaring at me for?" I bark as I land on the rug. "I had nothing to do with this."

He squawks in reply.

Hattie and Nana shush us at the same time.

I think I hear a little jingle as Merlin perches on the swing. I keep my eye on him. "Now stay in there!"

7

ALONE

Fenway!" Hattie yells.

What did I do? I hop onto the couch, leap over to the comfy chair, and scramble to the low table.

"FEN-way!" Merlin screeches.

I skitter to the end of the table, where Hattie catches me.

"Whew!" says Nana.

Hattie walks me over to the cage. "Friend," she says firmly, pointing to the bird.

Me? Friends with that mean bird? She can't be serious.

As if to show his agreement, Merlin turns toward the back of the cage. He tucks his head under a wing. Clearly ignoring us. Or sleeping.

For the rest of the morning, I follow Hattie and Nana around the house. They play the abracadabra game a few more times with scarves and cards and fake flowers. And no treats. Hattie smells happy even though the games don't seem very fun at all.

Later, Nana puts on shoes that make noise on the floor. Hattie brushes her bushy hair. My ears perk up. They're going somewhere in the car.

"Hooray! Hooray!" I bark, running in circles around them. "I love to go out in the car!"

"Aw, Fenway," Nana says, giving me a quick belly rub.

Hattie wags her finger at me. "Be a good boy."

Uh-oh. I'm getting a bad feeling about this. "I'm coming, too. Right, Hattie?" I bark, jumping on her legs. "You can't leave me here. Not with that bird."

But she doesn't listen. Nana grabs her keys and swings a bag over her shoulder, and the two of them head outside.

Without me.

"Wait! Wait!" I bark, pawing the door. I don't stop until I hear the car rev up and zoom away.

I turn around three times, then sink onto the mat. I curl up, my tail resting on my snout. This is not fair.

Maybe they won't be gone for long. Maybe they're coming right back. Maybe I won't even have time to close my eyes for a little rest before they—

"FEN-way! FEN-way!" comes from the big cage. I hear rustling and jabbing sounds. What a racket!

I try to ignore him, but it's no use.

"FEN-way! FEN-way!"

Why does Merlin have to be so loud? It sounds like he's freaking out in the cage. Is he mad at it or something?

I get up and trot toward the cage.

"Quiet down, loudmouth!" I bark.

I watch him flit back and forth and peck the metal bars. He's clearly upset about something. Is he just as sad as I am that Nana and Hattie left?

He knocks over his dish. He bobs his head against the water bottle. At least he's not ringing the bell.

Hey, where is that bell? It's not in the cage. It's supposed to be there, isn't it?

8

THE SEARCH

Merlin flies in circles. He bobs his head. He rattles his beak against the bars. "FEN-way! Bark-bark-bark!"

I shake my head a few times. Did that bird just bark like a dog?

"Bark-bark-bark!"

He did it again. I think he's trying to talk to me! But I can't understand him.

He's definitely upset. Maybe he's trying to tell me something. Hey, I bet I know what his problem is.

He wants that bell!

"Calm down, Bird," I bark at him. "You don't have the bell, but you do have a food dish and a water bottle. Why don't you play with those instead?"

Merlin doesn't seem to understand. Or maybe he doesn't want to listen. He keeps on fluttering around the cage, pecking and screaming. "FEN-way! Bark-bark-bark!"

I'm almost glad the bell is gone. That ringing hurt my ears. But the terrible racket the bird is making now is worse. He's zipping around like he's covered in fleas. Or being chased by a pack of squirrels.

I pace around the Lounging Place. This is the worst! If only I knew how to help him calm down.

I need a plan. And quick! But with all this commotion, it's hard to think.

The whole cage is rattling. Uh-oh. What if it tips over? Merlin isn't strong enough to do that. Is he?

All this trouble over a missing bell. It must be here somewhere. Wait a minute—I'm good at finding things. I'll sniff it out!

I rush back to the cage. I gaze up at him. "Listen, Merlin," I bark. "Just hold on a minute. I'm trying to help you."

"FEN-way! Bark-bark-bark!"

I'm not sure I really expected him to hold on, but it was worth a try.

I sniff across the Lounging Place floor, around the low table, and near the couch. When I get to the drapes, the scent of Merlin is un-mistakable.

His bell must smell like him. And that means it's behind the drapes! They're long and silky,  and their bottoms brush along the floor. Pretty dusty back here, too.

ACHOO!

I stick my snout under the drapes and root around. Besides dust, I  smell Merlin's aroma even stronger. Aha! I don't feel that bell, but my nose is telling me it's here somewhere.

I keep sniffing. I'm partway behind the couch when my nose taps something cool—*JINGLE-JINGLE!*

The bell!

I snap at it, but *JINGLE-JINGLE-JINGLE*. It's rolling away! *JINGLE-JINGLE-JINGLE!*

I go after it, squeezing between the couch and the wall. It's tight, but I won't give up. That bell cannot get away!

My nose taps the bell again, and I hear it roll some more. Maybe if I sneak up on it?

One more time and—*CHOMP!* I snag that bell in my jaws. I shimmy 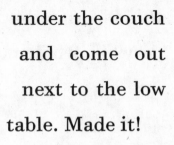 under the couch and come out next to the low table. Made it!

I want to call to Merlin, but my mouth is full. He's still making a racket in that big cage. "FEN-way! Bark-bark-bark!"

I leap onto the comfy chair and climb up the back. I'm as close as I can get. I wave my snout, showing him the bell. It rattles but doesn't jingle. Or ring.

He glances at me but keeps on flitting around and banging into things. And that's when I see the very big problem.

9

PLOP-JINGLE-JINGLE

How am I going to give the bell to Merlin? The big cage is still pretty far away.

I stretch up on my hind legs. I stick my snout out in the direction of the cage. I wave one of my front legs. But I can't reach it. Not even close.

What am I going to do?

Even if I could reach the cage, how would I open the little door?

The bird pecks the bars some more. He glares at me. He looks mad. "FEN-way! Bark-bark-bark!"

I sink onto my bum and think. I can't stretch far enough. I can't leap high enough. But maybe I can throw the bell back in there? Fetch Man makes it look so simple at the Dog Park. How hard can it be?

I sit up as tall as I can. I whip my head to the side and fling the bell forward—

It flies out of my mouth and—*PLOP-JINGLE-JINGLE*—lands on the floor.

Merlin reacts by pecking the bars. "Fenway!" he cries.

His voice actually sounds encouraging. Is he cheering me on? I scoot off the chair and down to the floor. I snag the bell, hop up, and climb onto the back of the chair.

Again, I rise up tall. I get a good grip on the bell. I whip my head to the side. I fling it forward and—

The bell sails out of my mouth. *PLOP-JINGLE-JINGLE*—it hits the floor.

Merlin slides his beak back and forth across the bars. "Fenway!" he cries in that hopeful voice again.

I think he really is cheering for me. "Okay, so that time didn't work, either," I bark. "But I'm not giving up."

"Bark-bark-bark!" Merlin flies around the cage in a wide circle. I can feel his energy urging me on.

I hop down and grab the bell again. I leap back up and perch on the top of the chair. This time, I rise up a bit taller. I get a better grip on the bell. I whip my head farther to the side. I fling the bell forward as hard as I can and—

It goes flying . . .

out of my mouth . . .
toward the cage . . .
and lands—*PLOP-JINGLE-
JINGLE*—right on top.

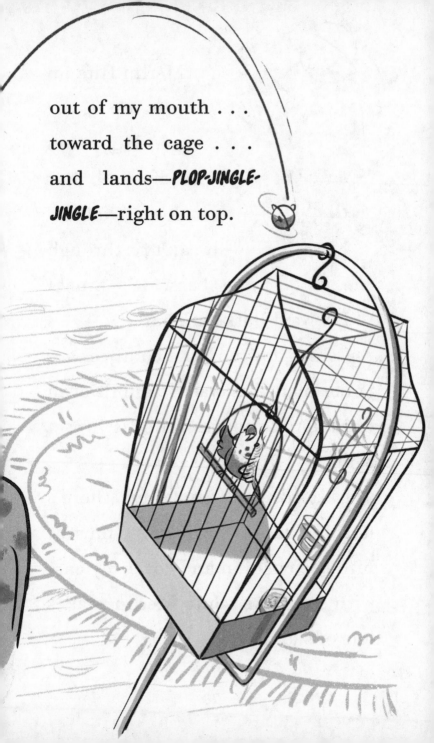

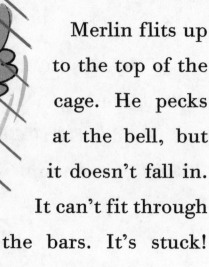

Merlin flits up to the top of the cage. He pecks at the bell, but it doesn't fall in. It can't fit through the bars. It's stuck!

"FEN-way! Bark-bark-bark!"

I slink down on the comfy chair. Some plan this was. It didn't even work! And now Merlin is upset again.

I tried to help, but there's nothing more I can do. I burrow into the cushion and cover my ears with my paws while Merlin makes lots of sad noises.

10

FRIENDS

It seems like forever before the front door swings open. Hattie and Nana are back!

I spring off the chair and rush over. "I'm so glad you're here!" I hurl myself at their legs. "I missed you so much." They smell like french fries and barbecue sauce.

Hattie rubs my head.

"Aw, Fenway," Nana says. She's holding a bunch of shopping bags. One of them smells delicious, like treats.

"FEN-way! Bark-bark-bark!" comes from the cage.

"Merlin?" Nana walks over. "What in the world? Are you barking?"

Me and Hattie hurry after her. Merlin is flying to the top of his cage and pecking at the bell.

CLINK-CLINK-CLINK.

"How did . . . ?"
Nana grabs the bell
and shows it to Hattie
like they've never
seen it before.

Or they're wondering how
it got there.

Hattie's shoulders go
up and down. So do her
eyebrows. She glances down at me.
"Fenway?" she asks.

I weave around their feet. "I
don't know why you're looking at
me," I bark. "That bell needs to
go back in the cage. And quick!"

Nana seems to get it. She opens

81

the little door. As Merlin flits back and forth, she latches the bell back in its place.

Merlin goes right for it. *DING-DING-DING!* And most importantly, his back end is waving happily like he's ready to play.

It worked! That dinging has never sounded so wonderful.

Nana claps her hands. "Give Fenway a treat," she cries.

Hattie scoots down and rubs my head. "Would you like that, Fenway?" she sings.

I jump up and spin. "Wowee! I love treats!"

The bell stops dinging. "GIVE FENWAY A TREAT," Merlin yells. "GIVE FENWAY A TREAT!"

"What a good idea!" I bark, leaping at Hattie's backpack. She swings it off her back, reaches in, and tosses a treat into my mouth.

CHOMP! MMMMM. "Hey, everybody!" I bark. "Let's play the abracadabra game—for real!" I rush over to Nana's scarf and pick it up. I drop it over the little ball on

the floor. I plop down beside it and gaze up at Hattie, my head cocked the way she likes.

Hattie claps her hands. Another treat appears.

"Abracadabra!" Nana cries.

Yippee! I could get used to this.

Me, Hattie, and Nana play the abracadabra game all afternoon. Then me and Merlin bark at squirrels. Now that he knows how to bark, he might as well put his skill to good use.

The next day, Fetch Man and Food Lady reappear. Hattie smells as sad as I feel when we say goodbye to Nana. And Merlin.

"I'm going to miss you, buddy," I bark.

"Give Fenway a treat!" he calls from the big cage.

Food Lady and Fetch Man gasp in surprise. Hattie and Nana just smile.

As we trot to the car, I think about friendship. It's like the ball in the abracadabra game. You might think nothing is there, but then *surprise*—you find it in the end!

ABOUT THE AUTHOR

VICTORIA J. COE's books for middle grade readers include the Global Read Aloud, Amazon Teachers' Pick, and One School, One Book favorite *Fenway and Hattie* as well as three Fenway and Hattie sequels. **Make Way for Fenway!** is her first chapter book series. Connect with her online at victoriajcoe.com and on Twitter and Instagram @victoriajcoe.

ABOUT THE ILLUSTRATOR

JOANNE LEW-VRIETHOFF's passion and love for storytelling is shown through her whimsical and heartfelt illustrations in picture and chapter books. Joanne also loves discovering the world with her family by traveling and collecting memories along the way, giving her more inspiration for her illustrations. Her favorite downtime activities are reading YA books recommended by her daughter, looking at TikTok videos of dogs and cats, and watching the Discovery Channel. Currently, Joanne divides her time between Amsterdam and Asia. Connect with her on Instagram @joannelewvriethoff.

LOOK FOR THE NEXT

MAKE WAY FOR FENWAY!

CHAPTER BOOK!

fenway
AND THE
GREAT ESCAPE